Chester

written by John Lockyer
illustrated by Kelvin Hawley

1

My puppy, Chester, wouldn't behave.
Every time I came home from school,
he was barking behind the door.
I banged on the door and shouted,
"Stop that noise!"

2

But Chester would not stop barking.
He made more and more noise.
When I opened the door, he always
jumped up and gave me a wet kiss.

When I played ball outside, I always
heard Chester scratching on the gate.
He shook the gate and I shouted,
"Stop that noise!"

4

But Chester didn't stop.
He scratched and barked louder.
When I opened the gate, he jumped
up and gave me a wet kiss.

In the middle of the night, I heard Chester howling in the kitchen.
I banged on the wall and shouted, "Stop that noise!"

But Chester didn't stop.
He howled louder and louder.
When I opened the kitchen door,
he jumped up and gave me wet kisses.

Chester would not behave.
One day when Mum came home from
the supermarket, Chester jumped up
and Mum dropped everything.

8

There were broken eggs on the floor.
Mum said, "Chester can't behave!
He needs to go to Dog School!
He will learn how to behave there!"

So, every Saturday, Mum and I took
Chester to Dog School in the park.
Soon he learned to sit and to stay.
Before long he could find and fetch.

He learned to lie down and roll over.
Mum and I found out some good
things, too. We learned to whistle to
Chester and to talk quietly to him.

On the last day at Dog School, there was a competition for all of the dogs. Chester was very good at everything. He ran through barrels and he jumped over high walls.

He went around the zig-zag poles.
He found my cap under some wood.
Then he found a ball in a tree.
He sat whenever he was told to sit.

Chester was the best dog of all.
He won a gold medal and a toy bone.
The instructor put the gold medal around
Chester's neck and he shook hands.

"Chester is the best dog," I said.
"Now he will behave," said Mum.
"Good dog," said the instructor, and
he gave Chester the toy bone.

When Chester saw the bone, his tail
hit the ground and his eyes rolled.
Suddenly, he barked and barked.
He jumped up and gave us wet kisses.
Chester couldn't behave!